Anthropology

101 true love stories

Dan Rhodes

CANONGATE
Edinburgh · New York · Melbourne

Thanks to: Tibor Fischer, Lawrence Norfolk, Sheenagh Pugh,
Tony Curtis, Stephen Knight, Christopher Meredith and,
particularly, W. B. & V. C. Rhodes.

First published in Great Britain in 2000 by
Fourth Estate, a division of HarperCollins Publishers

This edition published in 2005 by
Canongate Books Limited, Edinburgh

Printed in the United States of America

FIRST AMERICAN EDITION

ISBN 1-84195-649-X

Canongate
841 Broadway
New York, NY 10003

05 06 07 08 09   10 9 8 7 6 5 4 3 2 1

Contents

Anthropology

I loved an anthropologist. She went to Mongolia to study the gays. At first she kept their culture at arm's length, but eventually she decided that her fieldwork would benefit from assimilation. She worked hard to become as much like them as possible, and gradually she was accepted. After a while she ended our romance by letter. It breaks my heart to think of her herding those yaks in the freezing hills, the peak of her leather cap shielding her eyes from the driving wind, her wrist dangling away, and nothing but a handlebar moustache to keep her top lip warm.

Ashes

My girlfriend died. We hadn't been together long, and I had felt indifferent towards her. She left me her ashes. 'What should I do with them?' I asked her family.

'She wanted you to decide.' I really didn't care. 'You two were so in love; we're leaving it up to you to choose her final resting place.' They were incredibly compassionate, and the pressure was enormous. I found myself in a helicopter, scattering her over the meadow where she had ridden her pony as a girl. Her family watched, weeping their final goodbyes as the little grey flecks fell to earth.

Baby

My girlfriend's pregnancy lasted over two years. 'Maybe the doctor's right,' I said. 'Maybe a baby isn't going to come.' She wouldn't listen. She carried on buying nappies, teething rings, woolly hats and mittens, and little bits and pieces for the nursery. One afternoon I came home to find her cradling a bundle in her arms.

'Look,' she said. 'It's arrived. It's a boy, and it's got your eyes.'

'Well done,' I said. 'Congratulations.'

'And congratulations to you too. After all, you don't become a father every day.'

'I suppose not. But really it's you that's done all the hard work.'

Beauty

My girlfriend is so beautiful that she has never had cause to develop any kind of personality. People are always wildly glad to see her, even though she does little more than sit around and smoke. She's getting prettier, too. Last time she left the house she caused six car crashes, two coronaries, about thirty domestic disputes and an estimated six hundred unwanted and embarrassing erections. She seems to be quite indifferent to the havoc she causes. 'I'm going to the shop for cigarettes,' she'll say, yawning with that succulent, glossy mouth. 'I suppose you'd better call some ambulances or something.'

Binding

I found my girlfriend smashing our two-year-old's toes with a rock. I told her to stop. 'What are you doing?' I cried, above the baby's agonised wails.

'You wouldn't understand,' she said, winding a bandage tightly around the crushed digits. 'It's a woman thing. It'll help her get a boyfriend.'

'But darling, don't you remember what the doctor told us? It's a boy baby.'

'Really?' She looked surprised. 'Oh well. Men look nice with small feet too. I expect he'll be gay, anyway. He's got that look about him. See?' I had to agree that she had a point.

Blind

My girlfriend used my going blind as an excuse to start dressing sloppily. In the days when I could see her, she had always looked immaculate in the latest cuts of the best designer labels. Now, her high heels have been replaced by trainers, her silk stockings and short skirts by jeans, and her smart blouses and figure-hugging jackets by baggy jumpers. I haven't said anything yet, but it's getting to the point where I'm embarrassed to be seen with her as she gently holds my hand and guides me along, making sure I don't trip or bump into anything.

Bulletin

My girlfriend is so lovely that I can't help feeling sorry for all her ex-boyfriends. I'm sure they must spend all their time thinking about her and wondering what she could be up to. So every month I send them a bulletin detailing all the pretty things she has said and done. Sometimes I enclose a discarded pair of tights, or the stub of an eyebrow pencil. I feel I should do everything I can to make up for them having lost a girl with such soft brown hair, and whose feet are so small you can hardly see them.

Charging

My girlfriend started charging me for sex. She said she had to think of her future, and anyway her friends did it so why shouldn't she? I didn't mind too much because her basic rates were very reasonable, although she always expected tips for extras. Once, as she was holding the banknotes I'd given her up to the light to make sure they were real, I asked her if she ever went with anyone else for money. She was furious, and asked what kind of girl I thought she was. I said one with laughing eyes, and lovely long dark hair.

Chemicals

Unable to accept that Celestia was no more than a haphazard cluster of chemicals brought together by chance in a universe out of control, I started to believe. To give thanks for her pretty face and endearing ways, I've started getting up early and taking her from door to door, with a sign around her neck that asks: Am I just chemicals? 'Look at her,' I say to the bleary-eyed householders, 'and draw your own conclusion.'

Sometimes they chase us away, but usually they just mumble, 'She looks like chemicals to me,' and shut the door loudly in our faces.

Clever

Tabitha was declared a genius, and decided she needed more intellectual stimulation than I could provide. After weeks of searching, she found someone and brought him home. He looked far too handsome to be clever, but using words I could barely understand he told me I was history. The ravenous way Tabitha was kissing him suggested he had a point. She left me. For months I've lived in the hope of him being a useless lover, but yesterday she sent a fax telling me how much more accomplished he is than me at licking, fondling and many other matters of intimacy.

Club

Lulula got together with my friends' girlfriends, and formed what they called 'The Girlfriend Club'. They met regularly, and enjoyed themselves. We were delighted for them to be having so much fun, but were curious about what they got up to. They wouldn't tell us. Then one of the girls confessed in her sleep that these evenings were spent giggling, and looking at photographs of handsome, well-dressed men. Heartbroken, we implored them to disband. They wouldn't. Nowadays, whenever they get together we do as well, silently looking at pictures of their pretty faces as tears well up in our eyes.

Coping

My girlfriend left me, and I'm coping very well. Sometimes it's almost as though she hadn't run off with another man, and that she's still here with me. During the day I cope by imagining she's gone to the shop for some cheap cigarettes, and will be back at any moment, smiling with those lovely painted lips. When the shop's shut, I cope by telling myself that my favourite picture of her is real. I spend my evenings at the piano, singing love songs to her photographed face, and occasionally licking the black keys because they remind me of her skin.

Crying

My girlfriend left me, and I started crying in my sleep. My nightly lament became so loud that my neighbours called the police. The press found out, and people came to stand outside my house to hear me call her name and moan. Television crews arrived, and soon a search was on to find the object of my misery. They tracked her to her new boyfriend's house. I watched the coverage. People were saying they had expected her to be much more beautiful than she was, and that I should pull myself together and stop crying over such an ordinary girl.

Drawing

Paris had her bicycle stolen, and was never the same again. I try to visit her every month. Usually she is drawing intently, crayon on paper, confused crisscrossing lines which resemble nothing I have ever seen. 'That's lovely, Paris,' I tell her. 'What is it?'

'It's a bicycle.' Her pretty face lights up, and I remember why I fell in love with her. Then she looks away. 'I had one once.' She starts rocking slowly back and forth, tears streaming down her cheeks. I kiss her forehead, and return to my new love, who is aware of the situation and understands.

Drinking

I asked my girlfriend if she'd started drinking again. She said no. I searched her flat and found six empty three-litre bottles of White Lightning cider. 7.5%. When we met for lunch I showed them to her. 'What are these?'

'I don't know.'

'You must know. They were in your flat.'

She stalled. 'I didn't drink them.'

'Then who did?'

'No one. I used it as make-up remover.'

'All eighteen litres?'

'Yes.' She was wearing lipstick, and had mascara on the lashes of those innocent eyes. I told her she didn't need it; that she was pretty enough already.

Dust

Xanthe left me. I found out her new address, and returned the kettle she had left behind. The next day I took her a book she had lent me. I found a box of hairgrips, and delivered one each day. If she wasn't home I would post it with a long letter explaining how I had found it on the floor. When I had returned them all, I took her, on the tip of my finger, a tiny ball of dust. 'I remember seeing it fall from your dress one afternoon,' I said. 'The pretty one, with the flowers on it.'

Eggs

My downstairs neighbour seduced me so many times that when she started telling people she was my girlfriend I couldn't deny it. She moved her lipstick and dresses upstairs, and we shared the rent. I worried that I had been premature in letting her move in; after all, we hardly knew each other. When she called to tell me she had been arrested for tampering with the nest of a golden eagle, I was surprised. I began to wonder whether she was the right girl for me, but I'd become used to having her around, and anyway they were only eggs.

Endless

Often, one or other of Foxglove's ex-boyfriends will turn up on our doorstep bearing expensive eye-shadow. 'Will you give her this?' they choke. 'It's her favourite shade.' I take it. Then, heartbroken, they lash out. 'She'll leave you,' they cry, fists flailing. 'She thinks I'm the handsomest man in the world. She told me once, when we were kissing.' I hurt them as little as possible, but always make sure I win the fight. Sometimes, cigarette in hand, she'll come out to watch, smouldering as those perfect, endless legs vanish into the hem of her tiny brown suede skirt.

Expecting

With her long blonde hair, lily-white skin and Cupid's bow lips, Mariedel looks like an angel. Naturally I was delighted when she fell pregnant, but the baby's slanty eyes suggested she had been unfaithful to me. She apologised, and I forgave her. Soon the pretty thing was expecting again, and this child was nut brown. I didn't say a word. With the little mulatto cradled in her arms she looked so lovely that I just couldn't risk losing her. 'At last,' I said, 'a little baby of our own,' and one kiss from that perfect mouth made everything right again.

Exploring

I arrived at Zazie's deathbed to find her kissing her best friend's lips, and playing with her breasts. There was an awkward silence, then: 'I've always wanted to try it and I'm running out of time, so . . .' Neither girl could look me in the eye. 'She said she'd let me, and . . .'

'Well? Did you enjoy it?' I had to know. They looked uncomfortable. Then Zazie lifted her hand to her friend's face, and smiled. They giggled, and started exploring each other's bodies. I felt like an intruder. As, weeping, I left, her death rattle shook the room. I didn't look back.

Face

My girlfriend is so pretty that I can't get over it. Every week I celebrate the alignment of her features by parading a giant photograph of her lovely face around the town centre. I've written the words 'pretty face' on the picture's border, and drawn an arrow to direct people's attention towards it. It's not bragging, because it's her that's the pretty one, not me. I'm going to parade every week for as long as she lets me be her boyfriend, and probably even longer. Nothing's going to put me off, not even the shouts of 'had her' or 'been there'.

Faithful

My girlfriend died. I was heartbroken, and vowed to remain faithful to her memory. At first I had no difficulty; my distress was so great that I couldn't even contemplate kissing anyone else. But, after a while, another girl started showing an interest. I resisted her advances. 'You're very pretty,' I told her, 'but it's just too soon. I'm sorry.' She wouldn't give up. She kept gently touching me, and fluttering her mascara-coated eyelashes. Eventually I yielded, and fell into her arms. The man asked us to leave. He said our rustling, slurping and giggling was upsetting the other mourners.

Features

Jealous of couples with pet names for each other, we decided to think up our own. We racked our brains. Eventually, she came up with the name 'Femur' for me, after a childhood accident about which I had many stories. I settled on 'Girlfriend-features' because I couldn't think of anything else. Now, when we're with friends, we use our new names, and reprimand each other for doing so. 'Don't call me that when there are people around,' I say. 'Are you listening to me, Girlfriend-features?' She gives me one of her looks, but can't help breaking into a smile.

Fight

Azure lost her fight for life, and I gave a tribute at the memorial service. 'I know she was special to everyone here,' I choked, 'but she was very special to me because I was her boyfriend.'

A handsome, strong-jawed man stood up and shouted, 'No you weren't. I was her boyfriend.' Then a tall, almost swarthy man did the same. Before long there were eight of us, punching one another as hard as we could as the tears flowed down our cheeks. No one else got involved, or even seemed surprised. They just shook their heads and looked away.

Flowers

Tallulah lost control of her gambling habit. We lost our home, and started living in a tent. She still couldn't stop. To settle an argument with someone, she staked her waist-length blonde hair on a bet about the loveliness of the flowers in the park. The tension was too much to bear, but she won. The flowers were exactly as lovely as she had said. She showed me her prize. It was the loser's hair, in an old pipe-tobacco tin. It was short, grey and flecked with dandruff. It looked greasy, and neither of us wanted to touch it.

Friends

May Pang was keen for us to stay friends after we separated, and I agreed. She regularly calls at my house for coffee, often with her new husband in tow. When she left me I told her that it didn't matter and wished her well, so she thinks it doesn't hurt to have him around. Even so, they are careful to sit apart when I'm in the room, but when I go through to the kitchen to boil the kettle and choose which biscuits to serve, I can sometimes hear the soft slurp of kisses, and whispers of 'I love you.'

Fuji

Iolanthe is like Mount Fuji. From a distance she's majestic and alluring, but close to she somehow disappoints. I confide this to her suitors whenever they arrive with their roses and Spanish guitars. When she's out of earshot I tell them, 'If you seduce her away from me you'll be sorry.' They think I'm threatening them, but then I whisper, 'I know she's gorgeous, but when you get to know her she's really just an ordinary girl.' They ask why I don't leave her if this is the case. I stumble over my words. I just don't know how to explain.

Fun

My girlfriend started teasing me. At first I didn't mind her puffing out her cheeks to draw attention to my slight weight problem, or drawing pictures of my long-nosed profile on dusty vans. These days, as we walk along a crowded street, she will often joke in a loud voice about the frequency with which I find myself unable to bring her to pleasure, and how handsome other men are compared to me. People snigger behind their hands, and I try my hardest to laugh along. I don't want it to look as though I've got no sense of fun.

Glass

Tortoiseshell was sent to prison, and I went to visit her. I asked what she'd done wrong. She told me she'd been seen having sex in the street. 'That's funny, Tortoiseshell,' I said. 'I don't remember us doing that.'

'No, you wouldn't . . . I was with somebody else.' I was shocked, and she looked guilty. 'Do you forgive me?' she asked, looking terrific in her prison uniform, and pleading with her lovely heart-shaped face.

'Of course I forgive you,' I said. As my lips flew towards her, I broke my nose on the glass screen between us. She roared with laughter.

Groping

I invited my ex-girlfriend to the pictures, just as friends, and she said yes. During a particularly steamy kissing scene I couldn't resist taking a trip down Memory Lane by gently running my hand up and down the inside of her soft, bare leg. She ran screaming from the building. After the film I arrived home to find the police there, waiting to arrest me. I asked them why, and they told me I'd been accused of a groping offence. 'She never used to call it that,' I sobbed, trembling as they handcuffed me and led me to their van.

Herself

Running Water left me. She told me she was very fond of me, but that she needed some time to herself. Six weeks later I saw her outside the local church, wearing her very best ceremonial head-dress and clinging to the arm of an unusually handsome man. I rushed through the confetti, and glared at her. 'So how did you enjoy all that time to yourself?' I hissed.

'It was great, thanks,' she answered, smiling for the cameras, and looking even prettier than I remembered. 'I had two cups of coffee and a croissant, and then I read a magazine.'

History

As part of the getting-to-know-me process, Nightjar told me all about her ex-boyfriends. She went through her shoebox full of photographs. 'His penis was much bigger than yours,' she would say, 'but he had bad breath.' Or, 'He was quite old but he could still go all night.' When, at last, she had finished, she asked me about my romantic history. I told her I had been waiting all my life for that special someone, and how glad I was now I had finally found her. 'Ah. I see.' She rolled her eyes. 'You're one of those.'

Hobbies

My girlfriend had been unemployed for ages, so I was delighted when she finally applied for a job. She filled in the form in her best handwriting, but got stuck when they asked her to list all her hobbies. 'I've put smoking,' she said, 'but I can't think of anything else.' I racked my brains, but couldn't think of anything either.

'Well,' I said eventually, 'you could put sex. You enjoy making love to me, don't you?'

'No,' she said, chewing her pen. 'Not any more. I'll put hill walking. It's not as if they're going to check up on me.'

Honest

January said it was important for couples to be completely honest with each other, and I agreed. I told her very honestly how much time I spent thinking about her, that whenever I pictured the future she was always there by my side, and how even after three years together I sometimes couldn't help feeling a little nervous when she was around. She told me to stop. 'That wasn't what I meant,' she said. 'I meant I just don't love you any more.' She looked away. 'And the more I think about it, the more I realise I never really did.'

Horsebox

Although she's nearly twenty, Opal has an imaginary horse. When we met I was happy to join her in three-day-eventing on her lawn; jumping over tyres and saying 'giddy-up.' Now I'm starting to wish she would find another interest. So far this month I've bought her a riding hat, boots and a crop. She keeps suggesting we get a horsebox. 'Go on,' she says. 'Blaze needs one to get around in.' They're really expensive, but she looks so incredible in jodhpurs and with her hair up in a net that I'm finding it harder and harder to resist.

Indifference

Not wanting the intensity of my love to drive
Skylark away, I feigned indifference. I worried
that this tactic wasn't working; seeming bored
in my company, she would keep looking at her
watch as though impatient to go somewhere
far better. Even so, we would always dis-
interestedly arrange to meet up again. When,
besotted, I casually suggested we get married,
she shrugged her shoulders and, yawning,
said, 'Whatever.' I couldn't believe my luck.
The man asked us whether we were prepared
to love and cherish one another forever.
Skylark said she might as well, and I told him
I supposed so.

Innocence

I thought my beautiful fiancée was innocence itself until I met her parrot. She had taught it to say terrible things. Wank. Minge. Fist fuck. Stick it up your Jap's eye. I was disillusioned to find she had taken such delight in training an unknowing bird to swear. My love diminished, but I didn't cancel the wedding. The parrot was in the church. When the man asked whether anyone knew a reason for us not to marry, it squawked, 'Cunt flaps.' My bride bent double with laughter, and even though we made our vows I knew that the marriage was over.

Jam

The night before our wedding day, my fiancée and I had a romantic meal. She held my hand. 'Thank you,' she said. 'Thank you so much for marrying me. You're just so wonderful taking me on. Me and my three ugly children.' I was horrified. It was the first I'd heard of these three ugly children, and I wanted to know more. She explained that she hadn't told me about them in case they put me off her. 'Come and meet your new daddy,' she called, and they ran into the room. Their faces were covered in jam. They were horrible.

Kangaroo

Every day I find a new way of telling Tadhana how much I love her. I used to worry that she didn't believe me, so one evening she came home from work to find me wired to a lie-detector machine. Very sincerely, I told her just how much I cared for her, and how pleased I was with the way our relationship was going. This was verified by a series of bleeps. Today I gave her a life-size cuddly kangaroo. When she squeezes it, she activates a recording of my voice, crying: 'Please don't ever leave me. Please stay.'

Kiss

Kiss

Orchid is resolute that her first kiss be perfect. I took her to Paris in the Springtime. As we gazed across the Seine at the Eiffel Tower, I made my move. She pushed me away. 'No,' she said. 'It's just not romantic enough. I'm sorry.' I took her to a deserted, palm-fringed Bahamian beach, and her response was the same. I saved and saved until finally we stood at sunset before the Taj Mahal. 'It smells funny,' she said. 'It smells, and there's poor people everywhere.' I was disappointed too. The supposedly magnificent structure paled beside those untouched, velvet lips.

Kissing

Since the moment we met, my wife and I have not stopped kissing. I'm Catholic and she's Islamic, so there were complications. Throughout the delicate negotiations with our families, our lips did not part for a moment. Eventually they accepted our love, so we married. We walked, tongues tangled, down the aisle. Now, after six years of marriage, we are still fused. We had our first child without stopping kissing for the conception, pregnancy or birth. Our lips are four broken scabs, and our chins always covered in blood, but we will never stop. We are far too much in love.

Knife

Knife

I gave Lola a knife to use in the kitchen. Instead she had a lump of oak delivered, and began to carve. For days I couldn't work out what it would be, and she wouldn't tell me. She barely spoke, so intent was she on the task. It took shape. It was a man: taller, more handsome and far better endowed than me. She tells me she still loves me and that she knows he isn't real, but sometimes, as her long nails scratch my back and her white teeth gnaw my body, I swear I can hear her whisper 'Woody'.

Laughing

My girlfriend died laughing at one of my funny faces. Her friends were kind, and told me I shouldn't feel guilty; that she would have wanted to have died that way. They weren't there as her musical laughter turned to chokes, grunts and her death rattle. When I stopped grieving I found a beautiful new girl to love. She died laughing at a joke I made about her feet. The next one passed away similarly. My last girlfriend didn't die. She left me. She said we never had any fun together, that she wanted a man with a sense of humour.

Leaving

Badr-al-Budur told me she was leaving. The idea of either of us walking out on such a perfect romance was so funny I started to laugh. 'That's a good one,' I said, clutching my sides. 'You really had me going there, Badr-al-Budur.'

'No,' she said. 'I mean it. I'm really leaving. I'm sorry.' She grabbed her holdall, and rushed out of the house.

'Don't go,' I called after her, bending double and expecting her to scurry straight back in, smiling like a mischievous little pixie and dashing over to help me dry my eyes, which had filled with tears of laughter.

Lesbian

My girlfriend and I couldn't decide on a name for our little baby girl. Eventually she took her to the registrar, and said she would think of something on the way. When she returned, I was frantic with anticipation. 'So what's she called?'

'I called her Lesbian,' she said, smiling at the bundle in her arms. 'It's such a pretty name.'

I asked her what on earth had possessed her. 'Don't you know what it means?' She didn't, so I explained. The poor thing burst into tears.

'I didn't know there were ladies who did that to each other,' she sobbed.

Lilac

I was overcome with the desire to build. I bought bricks and cement and started work, going as high as I could. The tower was a little lopsided, and I tried to disguise this with thick layers of plaster. I painted it lilac, her favourite colour, as well as her name. I had not thought to dig deep foundations, and the clumsy oblong toppled in an autumn gale. These days it lies on my lawn, a haphazard pile of masonry. Hardly an appropriate tribute to one with such pretty lips, and whose kisses were so warm I can still feel them.

Lipstick

The police caught my girlfriend stealing money from a blind beggar. She kept silent, but they tortured her until she admitted that she needed it for lipstick. 'You have a job,' they barked. 'You can afford lipstick.'

'I can afford cheap lipstick, but it's horrible. It's soapy, and it never lasts.'

Fortunately, one of her interrogators was a woman. 'She's right. A girl needs to feel confident about her cosmetics.' They gave her a caution. As they released her the female officer, overcome with pity, slipped something into my girlfriend's pocket. A stick of Lancôme. Volcanique. It suits her very well.

Lost

My girlfriend was lost in space, and I was at my wits' end. Eventually her spaceship was located and brought down to Earth. I was euphoric. She was full of stories of how frightened she was when her circuit died, and how incredible it was to be in orbit. It was wonderful to hear, but she has been back for some time now and I wish she would change the subject. This morning she told me again that the Earth was about the size of a tennis ball, and the moon seemed much bigger and brighter than it ever had before.

Madrid

I was delighted to find a Spanish girlfriend, and celebrated our first anniversary with a surprise trip to her home city. I landed our helicopter in front of the Palacio Real, and took off her blindfold. 'Where is this?' she asked, in her lilting Iberian accent. I was surprised that she didn't recognise such a famous landmark, and suggested she ask a passer-by. She started crying. In a voice I didn't recognise, she told me she was sorry, that there had been a special offer on sunbeds, and it had seemed like the right thing to say at the time.

Me

Me

Emerald tried to go on holiday, but her bag was so big they wouldn't let her on the plane. She came home and I looked at what she had packed. I found the things I'd have expected: sun lotion, swimming costume, phrasebook. But most of her load was made up of pictures of me. She had packed framed portraits, several photo albums and a cushion on which she had embroidered my face. 'It would have been a whole week,' she sobbed. 'I had to.' I told her she didn't need to say another word, and kissed those soft lips until daybreak.

Memories

My girlfriend and I have been together for so long that every day is some kind of anniversary. Whenever she gets home, she finds me waiting with a surprise candle-lit meal. 'What is it today?' she asks, yawning after a tiring day at work. I gently stroke her face, and tell her that it's exactly three years since I thought up her pet name, Dimples, two years since our first pillow fight, or just one year since the night we tried to count the stars. She doesn't talk much during these meals. She's far too busy treasuring those golden memories.

Milestones

My girlfriend left me. I found she had been seeing lots of other men all along. She was loose, and I thought the world should know. I calculated the road distances from her house to over two thousand different locations around the country, and began to carve milestones. 'Mette's open legs: 263km.' That was the first one. I laid it on a verge just outside Ulfborg. After I had planted nine hundred and forty, I realised that it was not making me any happier, that I was carving them in heart-shapes, and that I missed her like nothing on earth.

Money

My girlfriend had always enjoyed showing off in front of foreigners, and when we met a Greek in a restaurant she swung from the ceiling fan. Amused, he increased its speed and she flew off, cracking her head on the floor. The Greek felt he should accept responsibility for her passing, and tries hard to compensate for my having lost such a lovely girl. Every month he sends drachmas or gold. My new wife feels funny about it, but that doesn't stop her spending it all on pretty dresses and paint for her face. She calls it her dead girl money.

Mould

I'm hopelessly in love with a bland girl. She has never said or done anything interesting. I spend hours trying to work out why I'm so deeply attached to her. I can't find the answer. Her hair is boring, her face is boring and her body is boring. Every time I come home from work to find her slumped on the sofa, surrounded by used yoghurt pots, my heart explodes and I feel giddy, like I'm walking on air. I take her lifeless hand, kiss her pale cheek and say, 'They broke the mould when they made you.' She rarely responds.

Museum

I turned our flat into a museum. Visitors are welcome to marvel at the daintiness of the pumps she left behind, and to look at the band with which she would tie her hair back from the face I kissed so many times. There are cabinets full of photographs, and letters she sent me. There's a framed birthday card on the wall, with three big kisses in silver pen. No one ever visits but I'm here every day, keeping my head as still as I can. I don't want to lose any of the brain cells that hold those precious memories.

Naked

Phuong's parachute failed to open, but she survived against all the odds. I visited her in hospital. She was entirely encased in plaster, except for her mouth. I asked her what had gone through her mind as she fell helpless towards the ground. Gently, she told me she had not given me a second thought; that she had only seen the face of her favourite radio star. Weeping, I asked her if there was anything I could do before leaving her life forever. She asked me to apply some expensive lipstick to her lips. She said she felt naked without it.

Nature

Amber suddenly discovered naturism. We went to the supermarket, and people couldn't help staring at her. She's very pretty, and the security guards were too shy to ask her to cover herself up. 'Darling,' I whispered, 'people are looking.'

'Let them,' she replied. 'I've got nothing to be ashamed of.' She told me she would leave me there and then if I didn't join her and stop wearing clothes. 'It goes against nature,' she explained. I took off my trousers, and the shoppers jeered at my skinny legs. When, at last, I took off my underpants they waggled their little fingers.

Noises

My girlfriend had been unemployed for ages, but eventually she found some work in an office. Although I couldn't find the courage to say anything, I was worried that her new role in life would come between us. She's been there some time now, and although she spends most of her working day furtively ringing me up to make kissing noises, I can't help feeling as though she's slipping away from me. The slurps from the other end of the line don't seem as passionate as they could be. It's almost as if her lips had other things on their mind.

Normal

After a blazing row, Harmony joined the nuns. 'That's it,' she said. 'I'm joining the nuns.' I was lonely and could hardly sleep, but three days later she escaped and came home. 'It was awful,' she said. 'We had to get up really early, and they made us wear horrible long black dress things and no make-up, and sing all these boring songs.' Thankfully things quickly returned to normal, and now she's back to spending her free time joining in with the adverts on TV, and making me get up from the sofa so she can look for her lighter.

Open

Melody suggested we begin an open relationship. Petrified of losing her, I enthusiastically agreed. These days I spend most nights alone on the sofa as she uses our bed to entertain her new boyfriends and girlfriends with rubberwear, bondage, coprophilia and DIY exhibitionism. Sometimes she asks me how I am finding our new approach to life and love, and I tell her that I like it very much. I daren't say that sometimes, as the low moans of a threesome fly from the bedroom, I catch myself wishing things could be just a little bit more like the old days again.

Ouija

Aurélia's experiment with herbal contraception failed, and we started expecting a baby. We were both very excited, and she was so impatient to meet the future member of our family that she decided to make contact through a ouija board. Wary of such things, I stayed out of the way, but when she had finished I was consumed with curiosity. 'So did the baby spell anything?' I asked.

'Well,' she said. 'He said he was going to be a boy.'

'That's wonderful. Anything else?'

'Yes.' Overcome with joy she sighed, smiled and patted her bump. 'He said, "Mummy I love you."'

Paint

My girlfriend is so besotted that she can't take her eyes off me. After we've turned out the light she puts on her night-vision goggles, and watches me as I sleep. Quite often I am woken by her sighing and her involuntary yelps of happiness. This has been going on for years, and is showing no sign of abating. Once I asked her to stop all this infra-red activity, but it didn't really work; I'd wake up to find her covering me in luminous paint, and softly whispering, 'Sometimes I wonder if you know how much I love you.'

Pieces

They kidnapped my girlfriend, and asked for an awful lot of money before they would even think about giving her back. I was grateful for the peace and quiet, so I wasn't in too much of a hurry to settle up. After a while they started posting me little pieces of her, starting with an ear in a soap dish. For some reason they aren't lowering the ransom. It doesn't make sense. They seem to think I'd pay as much for a girlfriend with no thumbs, ears, nose or nipples as I would for one with all her bits still there.

Pilot

My girlfriend had been unemployed for ages, so I was overjoyed when she found work as an airline pilot. She was excited, looked great in her cap and set off for Lisbon on her maiden flight. The silly thing was so busy fixing her lipstick in the rear-view mirror that she didn't notice her 747 heading straight for the Pyrenees. She ejected in time, but the passengers and crew perished. She lost the job, and is now back at home all day, eating cold baked beans with a knife, and trying to straighten her hair by pulling it really hard.

Plain

I've been seeing a plain girl for several years. Her mother enrolled in cosmetic surgery school, and we offered to help out. So, she's using my girlfriend as her final project, the idea being that she transforms her from a plain Jane into a textbook beauty. Now, when she walks around in obvious distress from her breast remodelling, black eyes peeping from her bandaged face, men approach her and give her their phone numbers. They are sure that when the swelling goes down she will look quite incredible. I hope her mother fails the course, that the project ends in disaster.

Plan

My girlfriend calls me The Man With The Plan, because I plan to marry her and for us to have children together. Once I asked her whether she'd ever made any plans. She said she'd always intended to make the most of her beautiful, soft young body by sleeping around. Then, when she was bored of that, she might begin to think about settling down. 'And when you do settle down,' I said, kissing and gently stroking her long brown hair, 'will it be with me?'

She rolled her eyes, curled her lip, and said, 'What kind of a question's that?'

Pneumonia

My girlfriend started coughing. Unable to bear the thought of her dying and leaving me to face the world alone, I rushed her to hospital. I demanded that they put her on a life-support machine. 'Quickly,' I screamed. 'Before it's too late.' The doctor told me she wasn't slipping away, that all she had was a little cold. I couldn't believe him. Before long we were surrounded by medical personnel. Jeering, and shouting terrible words, they chased us away. 'But what if it's terminal pneumonia?' I yelled, as stethoscopes and scalpels bounced off our heads. 'What would I do then?'

Precious

My ex-girlfriend and her new husband regularly stand outside my house, kissing and smiling at each other. I love her so much that I cannot ignore them. Every opportunity to see her is precious, and I press my face against the window. Sometimes they break off from their love play to look, point and jeer at me. Often her husband makes terrible signs with his fingers while my ex-girlfriend bends double, laughing hysterically as the tears stream down my face. The days we spent together were the happiest of my life, and I will always, always want her back.

Proust

I came home to find her packing. I'd had no idea things had gone wrong between us. 'I've been reading,' she explained. '"A cathedral, a wave of a storm, a dancer's leap, never turn out to be as high as we had hoped." That's why I have to go.' She patted my arm. 'I'm sorry.'

'But don't forget,' I blurted, '"All our final resolutions are made in a state of mind which is not going to last."' I was clutching at straws, and she knew it. She folded her pretty red dress, zipped up her holdall, and went without another word.

Pumpkins

I told Sapphire I'd always wanted to grow pumpkins; that my dream was to grow one so big that I could hollow it out and sit in it. Then, if it was watertight, I would climb in and float down the river on carnival day, waving to the children on the shore. She broke off from painting her long nails to tell me I'd be lucky to grow a pumpkin big enough for a dog, let alone a person, and that even if I could there would be no point. I decided she was right. I don't want to grow pumpkins.

Real

Angélique agreed to be my girlfriend. To celebrate I took her for a candle-lit dinner, and I had to keep pinching myself to make sure I wasn't dreaming. We started seeing more of each other. Before long, pinching stopped being enough, and I started sticking pins in my face. These days even pins can't convince me that she's really there. Every evening I prepare a romantic meal. As I gaze at her immaculately arranged hair and faultlessly made-up face, I carve chunks out of my flesh with a surgical saw. Somehow it still seems too perfect to be real.

Rehearsing

Mazzy started acting. Having such a pleasing face, she is always cast as the female lead. She rehearses at home. While I'm in the armchair watching television she's often sprawled on the sofa, perfecting the crucial clinch with her leading man. She tells me that her little gasps and sighs of pleasure are in the script. When I saw her in the park, writhing mouth to mouth with another man, I was upset and told her as much. She was indignant: 'Do you mind? We're rehearsing.' They went back to their rehearsal and I walked away, ashamed at having doubted her.

Sailing

My girlfriend cannot play the guitar. She strums slowly, erratically and woefully out of time. She sucks her lips in concentration, and sometimes stalls for as many as fifteen seconds between chord changes. When she stops playing, her eyes are bright with anticipation. 'OK. What was that?'

'I'm not sure. Was it "Moon River"?'

'No.' She looks disappointed. 'It was "We Are Sailing". You know, by Paul McCartney.' She starts another, and I know I won't be able to identify it, no matter how hard I try. This has been going on for seven perfect years. I hope she never learns.

Salesman

Tammy is a successful travelling salesman. Her job takes her away an awful lot, but I don't complain for fear of losing her. When she leaves she always looks very attractive in short, tight dresses and crimson lipstick. Often she's gone for days on end, and is too busy to call. I wish she would change her job. I'd like us to get married, and for her not to have to be away nearly so much. The lifestyle is bad for her. The hours are far too long, and she keeps catching venereal diseases from the toilet seats of faraway towns.

Saving

'I gotta go score,' my girlfriend would say at three or four a.m. She would return hours later, considerably out of pocket. She seemed healthy enough. Her eyes still sparkled and her cheeks glowed. 'You look well,' I would say.

'Thank you. I know.'

I told her I wanted an addiction too. 'We're a couple. We should do things together.' I pestered her until finally she confessed to never having taken heroin in her life. She wouldn't tell me anything else, but I looked everywhere and eventually found the money. She'd stitched it into the mattress, like a crazy old woman.

Schnauzer

For weeks I looked forward to our first Valentine's Day together, and could think of little else. When, at last, the special day arrived, she told me she'd been doing a lot of thinking, and had decided that it would be best for both of us if we were to go our separate ways. I was heartbroken, but I just had to give her all the gifts I'd spent so long preparing: red roses, champagne, perfume, Swiss chocolates, five gold rings and a schnauzer with a big pink ribbon around it. I'd been dying to see her little face light up.

Shipwreck

After the shipwreck I was devastated and cried for weeks. When I emerged from my grief I realised that my girlfriend's death shouldn't be the end of me. I found someone as pretty and nice as her, and eventually I invited her on a beach holiday. My old girlfriend was washed up on the shore. She'd been clinging to a plank for fourteen months, living on raw fish, rainwater and her love for me. I was faced with a choice. My new girl won because the old one was skinny and bedraggled, and besides, the water had made her all crinkly.

Shivers

My girlfriend is so in love with me I can hardly bear it. She's always telling me how manly my hands are, how attractive she finds my brow, and that the sound of my voice sends shivers right through her. Once, I tried to change the subject. 'Can we talk about something else for a change?' I asked.

'Of course we can't,' she said. 'How do you expect me to concentrate on anything else when you're there with your white teeth?' I closed my eyes and shook my head. 'Oh, do that again,' she cried. 'It makes you look so handsome.'

Sleeping

My girlfriend started falling asleep during sex. Disconcerted, I asked her whether I should be doing it differently or something. She told me everything was fine and that I wasn't to worry, but it kept on happening. Once, I shook her awake and begged her to tell me what it was she really wanted me to do. 'Oh, you wouldn't want to know,' she laughed. I told her I wanted to know more than anything in the world; that I could think of little else. She looked away. 'No, really,' she said quietly, almost to herself. 'You wouldn't want to know.'

Snakes

On returning from the Far East, my girlfriend decided to crouch on the pavement of the high street, selling terrapins and snakes. Trade was brisk, but she found herself in an awkward spot when a hungry python ate a passing child. The child's father was livid, and thrashed her so hard that she lost her sight. I hoped this would make her abandon her Oriental ways and settle into a more conventional lifestyle. Instead she reclaimed her old spot on the pavement, where she squats to this day, bellowing tuneless songs into an ancient microphone and hoping for low-denomination notes.

Special

My beautiful girlfriend and I are so at ease with our relationship that we feel perfectly happy to hold hands and kiss in public. When we see a person who looks a little lonely, we'll walk past them with our arms around each other, gazing contentedly into each other's eyes. If they don't notice us at first, we'll go back and stand directly in front of them, kissing passionately, sighing, and touching each other's bodies in the way only lovers can. It's so important for these people to see just how perfect life can be once you've found that special someone.

Spirit

My girlfriend awoke to find herself possessed by an evil spirit. The first thing I did was call an exorcist. He couldn't make it until the evening, so we waited. She threw things at me, cursed my name, kept trying to strangle me, and wouldn't let me kiss her. Really she was the same as ever, but at least she was no longer hellbent on bankrupting me and making me look inadequate in front of everyone. I started to prefer her this way. When the exorcist finally arrived, I sent him away. I told him it had been a false alarm.

Squeals

Within minutes of meeting my fiancée I realised we were incompatible, but by then there was no turning back. So delighted to have met me, she immediately started making wedding preparations. I tried to think of a way of telling her it would never work, that I could never love her, but my mind went blank. Carried away by the moment she kept smiling at me, sighing, patting my hand and excitedly biting her lip. Delirious, she called her mother to tell her the good news. She told her I was Taurean, and I could hear the maternal squeals of delight.

Straight

When we started seeing each other, Miracle told me it was no big deal, that we were just friends who happened to be spending some time as lovers. Eventually, though, we moved in together and started a family. Seven years and three beautiful children later, she suddenly announced that she was leaving, that she had found somebody new. Between sobs I told her I felt let down and betrayed.

'Oh, come on,' she snapped, rolling those lovely, limpid eyes and shaking her head in disbelief. 'Don't give me all that. Are you seriously trying to say I wasn't straight with you?'

Stuff

Treasure left me. 'I'm so sorry,' she said. 'I understand how awful you must feel.' Choking, I told her she couldn't begin to understand. She insisted that she could. 'You know you'll never find anyone as pretty as me,' she explained, 'or as nice, and your every moment will be clouded by nagging recollections of times we spent together; times when you wrongly believed we had some kind of future. Believe me, I understand,' she said, gently. 'A part of you has died, the part capable of loving and trusting, and you know you'll never get it back. Stuff like that.'

Support

Tired of her ex-boyfriends desperately trying to get back with her, my girlfriend arranged a support group for them. When she told me she loved me very much, but only as a friend, she gave me their number and I went along. We meet every week. Sitting in a big circle, we try to get over her by talking about other things. It isn't easy. Every subject we try seems to return to the warmth of her naked body beside us in the morning, or the way she flicks her hair away from her face as she smokes a cigarette.

Sushi

My town has a university, so for nine months of the year there are pretty Japanese girls everywhere. I like to watch them as they walk around. With their little smiling faces and shiny black hair, they seem like such nice people. There's one that's my favourite, and every time I see her I approach her and ask for a quick language lesson, or ask her whether she knows a good place to eat sushi. So far I have learned all the numbers up to twenty-three, and been told several times that the nearest Japanese restaurant is some way away.

Tagged

When we started getting serious, I had my girlfriend electronically tagged. She thought this was terribly romantic, and whenever my radar device brought me to her work, the park, a café or a friend's house, she greeted me with a delighted smile and a long, gentle kiss. Lately I've started to worry that she's unwell. When I track her to the pool or the train she appears less surprised, her smile lacks its former dazzle, and her kisses leave my cheek much sooner than before. She seems distant and thoughtful. She really isn't herself. I think she should see a doctor.

Taxidermy

Columbine broke her neck by mistake. I took her to the taxidermist, and they delivered to my house a fortnight later. When I unwrapped the package I found the wrong girl. I reached for the telephone, but something stopped me. I looked again. The girl was pretty. Her hair was longer than Columbine's; her cheekbones more regal. I placed her in the diorama I had already prepared. Her boyfriend found out and came round for her, but I gave him some money and he went away. He told me she had been Australian, and that he had never really liked her.

Together

Hummingbird is the answer to my prayers. We spend our evenings kissing and gently stroking each other's skin, but this idyll is always shattered by a phone call from one ex-boyfriend or another. In mortified chokes they tell her how much they still love her, and how unbearable the pain is, sometimes even several years after the break-up. Hysterical, they beg for her to take them back. She listens politely, tells them to pull themselves together, and puts the phone down. 'That'll be you one day,' she purrs, and kisses me so sweetly that it almost breaks my heart.

Toys

On the last day of our relationship, my girlfriend brought toys. I had no idea our romance had ended, and was delighted to join her in a Connect 4 contest. 'It's over,' she told me, halfway through a game.

'What's over?' I asked, happy to be having so much fun.

'You and me,' she replied, abandoning Connect 4 and plugging in Astro Wars. 'I don't want to see you any more.' I tried to see how much she was scoring, but was blinded by tears. I knew the game, and just by listening I could tell she was doing very well.

Tractor

My girlfriend waited until I'd finished fixing her tractor before telling me we had no future together. I was knocked for six, and begged for an opportunity to talk things over. She told me she had made up her mind, and that nothing I could say would change it. I continued to plead, but she just put on her ear-muffs and drove away. I called after her, my voice hoarse with emotion, 'Think of all the happy times we've spent together.' I don't think she heard me. She just kept on driving, her golden hair glowing in the evening light.

Travel

Every day I send Lucia a photograph of myself. Sometimes the shot will include a recent newspaper to prove that it's up to date. Just lately I've started travelling around the world. Sobbing, I'll ask a fellow tourist to photograph me at Golden Gate Bridge, the Acropolis, or the mud-palaces of Mali, and in every shot I'm visibly distraught. She said she was sure I'd get over it in time, but I know I never will; that no matter where I go, all I will ever really see is her lovely guilty face telling me she had found somebody new.

Trick

My girlfriend told me she had been the victim of nature's cruellest trick, that although born male she had always felt female. She said she had started dressing in women's clothes at the age of seventeen, and three years later had undergone the necessary surgery. I was stunned, but told her that I loved her first and foremost as a person, and that I would give her all the emotional support she needed. She looked horrified. She had only been joking. She left me. She said she was going to find a real man, not some queer little gayboy like me.

Trouble

My girlfriend and I have been sharing a flat for several months. Most mornings she asks me whether I would like something to drink. 'We've got tea or coffee,' she says.

'I'm fine,' I say. 'Really.'

'But it's no trouble. I'll be having something myself. Which would you prefer?' I tell her I prefer coffee, but that I'm really not thirsty. 'But you've got to have something before you go to work,' she insists, looking intently at the kettle.

'OK, I'll have a coffee,' I say reluctantly, my body screaming out for caffeine. 'But only if it's not too much trouble.'

Truncheon

My girlfriend joined the police without telling me. I didn't find out for two years, and then I came across a truncheon in the magazine rack. Confronted with this evidence she blushed, stammered and looked so pretty that I forgave her. She put on her uniform, and it was like falling in love all over again. I kissed her, and she kissed me. Together we walked into the bedroom. I began to undress. The moment I took down my underpants she arrested me for indecent exposure. She gave evidence against me in court, and I served six months. She didn't visit.

Video

After Firefly left me I presented her with a video recording I had made of myself, so if she ever felt down she could be reminded that there was somebody out there who loved her more than anything in the world. I met her in the street, and asked her if she ever watched it. She said she did, and that it always cheered her up. She told me she particularly liked the part where I kissed and caressed the tiny black skirt she had left behind, and cried like a new-born baby. She said that always made her smile.

Violins

Petrified at the thought of age withering my boyish good looks, Sundial blinded herself with a soldering iron. 'You're handsome today,' she tells me every morning, dark glasses hiding the mess in her sockets. 'Every time I'm near you I hear violins.'

'But how do you know I'm so handsome, Sundial?' I ask, as I pat her hand and run my fingers through her hair. 'You can't see me any more.'

'Oh, I just know you are. It must be those violins. Sometimes I wish they'd shut up.' She flashes me an impish smile, so I know she doesn't mean it.

Volcano

The volcano erupted. Wanting our love to be preserved forever, we stood outside and started kissing. Everyone else fled for cover, but not us; we wanted to be petrified by the ash, so future generations could visit us and see how special we were to each other. However, the volcano wasn't as destructive as everyone had anticipated, and we survived with extensive burns. Even so, people come to look at us, and to marvel at our devotion. They ask us to kiss for them. They take photographs, as the reptilian moonscapes where our faces used to be join together in love.

Well

My girlfriend left me. I tried getting on with life, but it just wasn't possible. After eight years of sleepless, tear-soaked nights I went to the town she had moved to, hoping to see her. When, finally, she appeared, I rushed up and said hello. She looked puzzled. 'You don't remember me, do you?' I said.

'No.' She shook her head. 'I'm sorry.'

'But we went out,' I said, as if it didn't really matter. 'I kissed your lips.'

'No, I can't remember. But never mind all that,' she said. 'How are you?' I told her I was very well.

Words

I fell in love the moment I saw her in her grandfather's kitchen, her dark curls crashing over her Portuguese shoulders. 'Would you like to drink coffee?' she smiled.

'I'm really not that thirsty.'

'What? What you say?' Her English wasn't too good. Now I'm seventy-three and she's just turned seventy. 'Would you like to drink coffee?' she asked me today, smiling.

'I'm really not that thirsty.'

'What? What you say?' Neither of us has the gift of language acquisition. After fifty years of marriage we have never really spoken, but we love each other more than words can say.